How Many Ants?

by Larry Dane Brimner
illustrated by Joan Cottle

Children's Press®
A Division of Grolier Publishing
New York • London • Hong Kong • Sydney • Danbury, Connecticut

For Shirley Mullin and Kids Ink
— L.D.B.

For my Mom and Dad, with love
— Joanie

Reading Consultant
Linda Cornwell
Learning Resource Consultant
Indiana Department of Education

Library of Congress Cataloging-in-Publication Data

Brimner, Larry Dane.
How many ants? / by Larry Dane Brimner ; illustrated by Joan Cottle.
p. cm. — (Rookie reader)
Summary: Ants increase by multiples of ten as they march up the hill toward a tall cake.
ISBN 0-516-20398-3 (lib.bdg.)   0-516-26251-3 (pbk.)
[1. Counting. 2. Ants—Fiction.] I. Cottle, Joan, ill. II. Title. III. Series.
PZ7.B767Ho 1997
[E] —dc21
96-37934
CIP
AC

Ten ants marching.

Twenty ants marching.

Twenty ants and ten.

Marching. Marching.
Marching up a hill
toward a tall, tall cake.

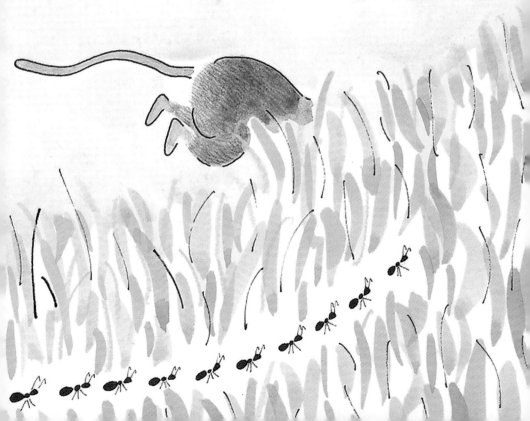

9

Forty ants marching.

30 + 10 = 40

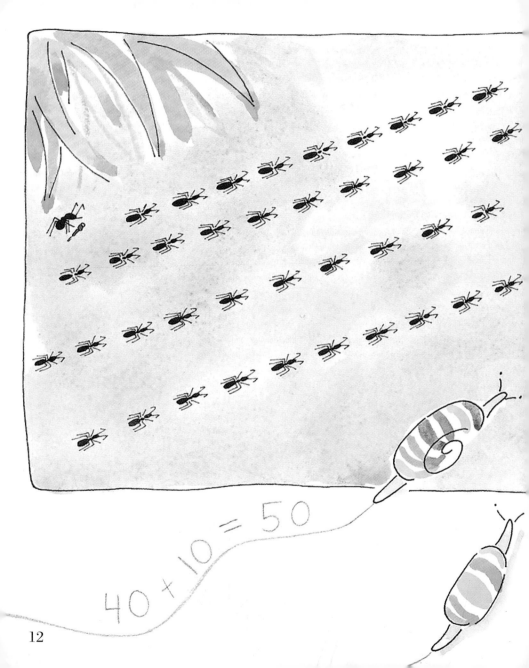

40 + 10 = 50

Fifty ants marching.

Fifty ants and ten.

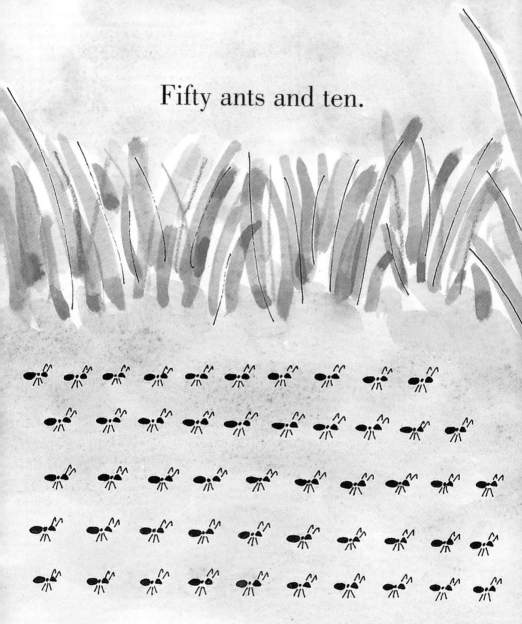

Marching. Marching.
Marching by a lake
toward a tall, tall cake.

Seventy ants marching.

Eighty ants marching.

21

Ninety ants and ten.

Marching. Marching.
Marching over leaves
toward a tall, tall cake.

What cake?

The tall, tall cake
that Sam and Al just ate.

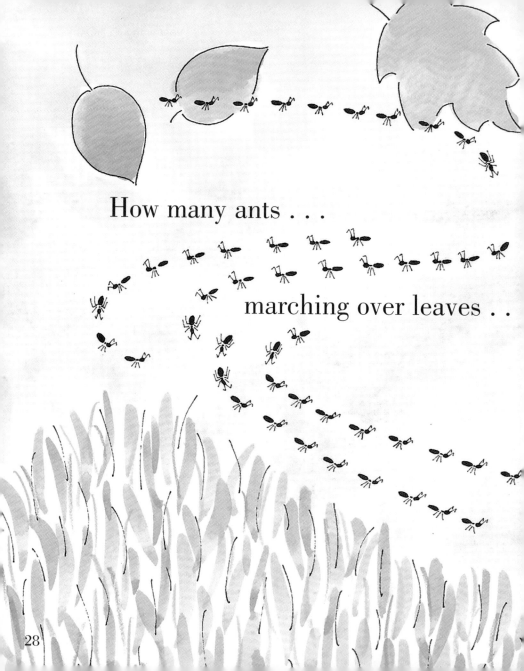

How many ants . . .

marching over leaves . .

marching by a lake . . .

marching down a hill?

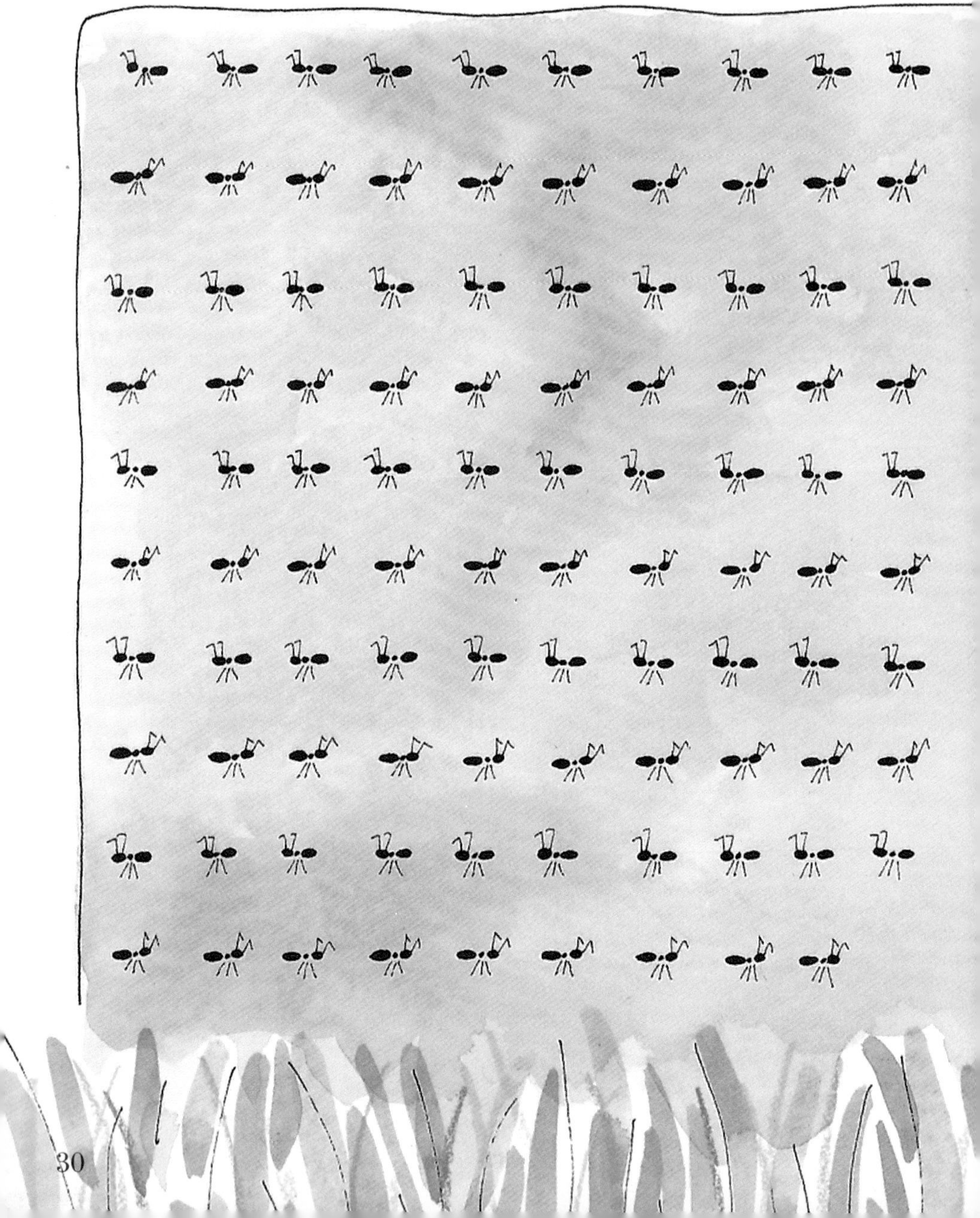

One hundred ants . . . too late!

About the Author

Larry Dane Brimner has always had an active imagination. Growing up on Kodiak Island, Alaska, and in rural southern California, playmates were few and far between, but his imagination solved that problem. His stuffed animals might become a class of students for him to teach. (As an adult, Larry taught school for twenty years.) His bicycle might at one moment be a snazzy little roadster and the next, a limousine. (Today, Larry usually drives an old Jeep around the Southwest.) A towel safety-pinned around his neck allowed him to take flight. (Now, Larry uses commercial planes to fly from city to city to speak to young authors about the writing process.) And a runner on a split-rail fence might be a high wire on which he could perform. (With age and accompanying wisdom, Larry prefers to keep both feet planted on the ground, though he sometimes spends his free time mountain biking or rock climbing in the Colorado Rocky Mountains.)

Larry is the author of more than forty books for young people. His most recent Rookie Reader titles include *Firehouse Sal* and *Brave Mary*.

About the Illustrator

Joan Cottle grew up in Connecticut and studied fine art at Boston University. She now lives in Los Gatos, California, with her husband, two children, and yellow lab. To illustrate this book, Joan happily painted more than 1,050 ants, 2,100 antennae, and 6,300 ant legs!